Dog Days

Dog Days

by Bernice Myers

Illustrations by the author

A
LITTLE APPLE
PAPERBACK

SCHOLASTIC INC.

New York Toronto London Auckland Sydney

Cover illustration by Carol Newsom

ISBN 0-590-42302-9

12 11 10 9 8 7 6 5 4 3 2 1   9/8 0 1 2 3 4/9

Printed in the U.S.A.   28

First Scholastic printing, June 1989

To Alyse
and
To Marc

♡

1

From time to time my parents talk about getting a watchdog — a dog that will bark like crazy when someone gets within five hundred feet of our front door . . . kind of a four-legged alarm system. Which sounds great to me as long as they promise to take care of it themselves. But since they both go to work, who do you think will end up with the job? It won't be Uncle Louie in Louisville.

Now, I'm really a very busy guy with a very busy schedule. What with going to school, homework, keeping my room neat, baseball practice, visiting relatives, brushing my teeth, plus a hundred other things I do every day, a dog would be just one more chore. He'd have to be walked, washed, brought to the vet, petted, played with, chased after, fed. . . . It might not seem like such a big deal, but if you add up the amount of hours, it would cut my free time by half.

Don't get me wrong. I really love animals — but on somebody else. When I feel like playing with a cat I go to Marilyn's house. My friend David has a St. Bernard. When I want to kid around with a dog, all I have to do is ring David's doorbell, and Igor comes charging out at me. We wrestle around a while, and then I get up and go home the way my grandpa does with me.

So it really shook me up when my mom announced that she and Dad were going to buy *me* a dog for *my* birthday.

"No," I said emphatically. "No pets of any kind. Dogs included. I don't want a dog for my birthday or for any other day. And that's final."

My parents fell silent. Nothing more was said about it for a long while . . . almost ten minutes. They began again as I bit into a hero sandwich. They pleaded with me to let them buy me a dog.

"But I don't want a dog," I said. Mom tried tears. But I was determined not to give in.

"It's impossible," I insisted. "Just get me the computer I asked for, and I'll forget this whole incident ever happened." They seemed to have accepted my final word . . . it wasn't mentioned again.

But life at home took a strange turn. For instance, at dinner I left all the string beans on my plate as I usually do — but no one made me eat them. It upset me. Really bothered me. I get worried if I'm not yelled at when I'm supposed to be.

There were other things as well. One

morning I found my father making my bed.

Of course he might have thought he was making *his* bed, but that would have been even more strange — he *never* makes his bed.

Then there was the toothpaste spread neatly on my brush and my schoolbooks all packed and waiting for me on the desk. By now I was completely confused and also late for the school bus, which was just passing by the living room window. I made a dash for it, but the bus was already blocks away, and I ended up late for class. Go explain to my teacher, Mrs. Attard, what kind of life I was leading at home.

2

No baseball practice today, which means I have a whole two hours to spend as I like. I walk through the park, taking the long way home.

I drop my books off at the house.

"Mom! Mom, where are you?"

I found her in my room, looking like the cat that swallowed the canary. I knew why right away. All my clothes had been picked up from the floor — and after all the trouble I went to to throw them there! If I had wanted to, wouldn't I have put them in the hamper myself?

"Uh, thanks, Mom. Thanks." It was obvious my parents wanted something from me . . . and I knew what! But nothing prepared me for the evening meal . . .

pizza, ice cream, chocolate cake, and mashed potatoes. (I like mashed potatoes as much as ice cream, as nutty as that sounds.)

Mom is smiling at me; Dad tucks a napkin under my chin. I expect him to move my jaw up and down next. Mom says, "Enjoy," and I do. Each time I look up from my plate they're smiling at me. Normally they never smile at me when we eat. In fact, they're usually complaining about something wrong that I'm doing . . . or not doing. I could feel the tense vibes around the table.

Then Dad spoke to Mom.

"Dear," he began. (Dear is my mother's other name. Dad alternates between Mary and Dear, depending upon what he says next. Like if his cuff links are missing he calls her, "Mary!" On the other hand, if he wants Mom to sew on a button, he says, "Dear." Anyway, that's not the point.)

"Dear," my father began. "Reney Disher told me today that he and Gert just bought Danny a beautiful Airedale for his birthday."

My jaw fell open. Pieces of chocolate cake cascaded down the front of my shirt. "Danny! A *dog!*" And after he and I swore an oath in blood that neither of us would ever get involved with pets of any shape or size! I was so upset I couldn't even finish my dessert. My mind was reeling.

"Isn't that nice," I heard my mother answer. "It's funny because I met Mrs. Ames in the library today. Her dog had puppies and she wanted us to have one . . . free. Imagine. A pure thoroughbred, too."

I asked to be excused from the table. Enough is enough. I dialed Danny's number. His mother answered. "I'm sorry, Benjie, but he's out walking his dog."

His *dog*? I ran out the door and over to his house. Danny was coming toward me. Until now he and I were about the only kids left who had not given in . . . not surrendered. And for similar reasons.

Danny knew what I was getting ready to say. He spoke first.

"I couldn't help it. I was in a weakened condition from all the exams," he pleaded. Poor Danny. But, if *he* had fallen into the trap, how long would it be before I'd be joining him?

3

I couldn't sleep much that night. I knew the pressure on me would get worse. They'd catch me in a weak moment and I'd end up walking a dog. Never! Never! NEVER!!

The next day was Saturday . . . only a week left until summer vacation. Mr. Label, the baseball coach, picked me to play on the team this year. I got dressed in my new uniform, ready for first-day practice.

Breakfast was chocolate cake again. I

was getting sick and tired of it. I yearned for a healthy bowl of oatmeal with milk and orange juice. Oh where, oh where were the good old days? Tell your parents you like something, and they feed it to you forever.

Faint barking was coming from somewhere. It sounded like it was coming from the basement.

"It must be Danny's new dog," Mom said quickly.

"Yes, yes, that's it," Dad said, choking on his toast. "It's certainly Danny's new dog, isn't it, Mary?"

"Yes, Honey, I'm sure it is." (Mom sometimes calls Dad "Honey." His other name is Al.)

Dad began having a coughing fit and excused himself from the table. "Gotta go to work."

"It's Saturday," I reminded him.

"So it is, so it is." But he left the table anyway. And Mom followed seconds after him. "What's going on?" I wondered. "The house is going to the dogs."

When I realized what I had said I laughed like crazy and tried to think of other sayings. What is it my father always says? "It's a dog-eat-dog world." "Love me, love my dog." "Let sleeping dogs lie." "A dog's bark is worse than his bite." Now that one's only true half the time. In fact, my friend Tommy will tell you that a dog's bite is much worse than his bark. He had to have twelve stitches in his leg last year when a barking dog bit him in the leg.

"Mom. I'm going out. I'll be back for lunch."

"Please don't slam the . . ."

Too late. I opened the door and yelled in, "Sorry." This time I held the knob and closed the door without so much as a click.

What a great day. Sunny and cool. Just right for nine innings. When I turned the corner Danny was sitting on the steps of his porch. His dog was racing around with a stick stuck between some mean teeth.

"Hi, Danny, aren't you coming to BB practice?" (I love reducing words to initials.)

"I'll be there as soon as I'm finished walking Sally here. . . ."

So what else is new? The park is about a five-minute walk away. "Hey, Gussie, how ya doin'?"

"Great! Watch this trick my dog can do. . . ."

Who cares?

Nicky is at the ballpark, already.

"Hi, Champ. Pitch me couple, will ya?"

Nicky always calls me "Champ." He knocks off a few outfielders. With the team we have this year I was almost positive we could win the championship game at the end of summer. The others were beginning to arrive.

"Hi, Jonathan."

"Hi, Benjie."

"Hi, Danielle."

"Hi, Greg."

"Hi, Jonathan. Hi, Champ. Hi, Nicky."

"Hi, Bonnie."

"Hi, Greg."

"Hi, Benjie."

Mr. Label arrived last.

"Hi, gang."

"Hi, Coach." Today he wasn't alone. He had his dog with him and tied him to a tree.

"Okay, guys. Play ball."

4

School was over, finally, and everyone took part in the yearly ritual . . . tearing up our notebooks and throwing them in the air.

I ran home with my report card clutched in my hand, hoping the two A's would offset the three C's that I got.

Mom was waiting for me at the door.

"Benjie, Mr. Label just stopped by. He wants to talk to you about something."

I rode my bike over to his house. He probably wants to tell me he has another pitcher. Or maybe he doesn't want me on the team at all. He could have telephoned me or sent his dumb dog over with a message. . . .

By the time I reached his house, I had all the answers worked out.

"Mr. Label, I'll practice an extra hour a day. . . . "

"That's great, Benjie. Come in." And then he hit me with it. "We're going away for a week tomorrow, and I wonder if you'd take care of Sandy for us till we get back. He's a good dog and you'll just have to feed him once a day and take him for a walk a couple of times a day."

You could have knocked me over with a feather. So this was why he wanted me. Would I say no about anything to my baseball coach? "Sure, Mr. Label. Great!

I'd love to. No problem. Nice doggie. No need to pay me. Naa, no trouble at all. A pleasure." (At this rate I'll never get to heaven.)

"I'll be back for Sandy tomorrow," I said. I got on my bike and headed for home.

First day of vacation and I'm tied to a dog for a week! What luck. I had to cancel all the arrangements I made with Danny and Jackie and David and Greg.

"Hello, Greg? I can't go to the beach with you Wednesday. I'm taking care of the coach's dog this week. What's so funny? Hey, don't be a wise guy. Cut it out." I banged down the receiver. The first casualty of the week. Mad at me for life.

I went through the rest of the day in a daze, trying not to think of tomorrow. If I didn't think about it, maybe it wouldn't come.

5

But come it did. Right after I woke up. There it was: Day one.

I got dressed and went over to the coach's house with my wagon. I wheeled the doghouse back to my yard. Then I went back for the dog.

The coach said, "His name's Sandy." (I already knew that.) "He'll help you with your pitching. Toss a curve ball and he'll run and bring it back."

"Don't worry," I heard myself say, "he'll be just great. Have a good time. Good-bye."

I brought Sandy home with me, and, of course, my mother fell in love with him right away. "Isn't he beautiful! And so handsome!" Sometimes Mom tends to go overboard.

Well, here we are, the perfect couple . . . boy and dog. Sandy was racing back and forth through the house, jumping up on me, licking my face, running to the other end of the house. . . . After about four repeats I took him outside and tied him up to the doghouse. He barked a lot but soon settled down and went off to sleep. I wasn't exactly full of energy myself anymore. That was the most activity in our house since a mouse entered our kitchen by way of the window.

Since today was Sandy's and my first

day together, I wasn't sure yet what signals to look for when he had to "go," so I walked him outside five times.

I liked the way he pulled at the leash and the feeling of power I had trying to restrain him. Man over dog. Strong over weak. Big over little.

By evening I gave him some dried stuff,

dog Cracker Jacks, which he crunched between his teeth. When he finished he walked over and lay down next to me at the TV. I stroked his back and rubbed his ears. What a picture we must have made as Dad came in the door.

"What's this, what's this?"

"It's Sandy. My coach's dog. They went away for a week and I'm taking care of him."

A grin slowly made its way across my father's face. . .almost to his ears. "Well, well, well," was all he said before sitting down for dinner.

I took Sandy outside to his house for the night. "Only six more days to go," I said to him, meaning every word.

6

In the morning, rain was coming down in buckets. I rolled out of bed and landed on the floor. "I hope Sandy's all right down there in the yard. He's probably fast asleep in the doghouse . . . smart dog."

A sudden clap of thunder sent me back into bed. A flash of lightning chased me under the covers. I wondered how Sandy was taking all this. . . .

The rain was coming down harder than ever. I couldn't stand it anymore. I got dressed and ran out to the doghouse.

"Here, Sandy," I urged. "Here, boy." But he wasn't there. Then where was he? I made a slow 360-degree turn. Nowhere, that's where.

I tried to think where I would go if I were a dog, but all I could think was, The butcher.

"Here, Sandy. Come on, boy. Look what I have for you-u-u-u." I walked through the streets for hours, calling him and getting nowhere. I was scared. What if the dog catcher finds him and brings Sandy to the pound? What if nobody claims him and they decide to put him to sleep? That really made me panic. "Sandy. Sandy. Come home. Please come home. . . . "

By late morning I was exhausted and soaking wet. I headed for home. What would I tell Mr. Label? Would he throw me off the team? Was I in a jam!

"Hi, Benjie." It was Danny.

"Did you see. . . ?" I didn't have to finish the sentence. There was Sandy with Danny's dog.

"Sandy!" I shouted as I ran toward him. But he bolted and ran in the other direction.

"He thinks you're playing with him. Just stand still and he'll come to you," Danny said.

Sandy eyed me from around a corner. Then he ran toward me and stood rigid about fifteen feet away. He was panting, and his tail was swinging like a conductor's baton. Then he made a final dash toward me, and I was able to grab the leash. "See ya, Danny," I said and raced Sandy back home.

I tied Sandy up to the doghouse as tightly as I could, making sure his adventures were over forever. While I was stroking his wet fur I could feel his heart beating like mad. "Why did you run away?" I asked him. "You could at least have waited until you heard me practice my violin."

What a day this was! It was almost over.

Mom was making dinner and Dad was coming up the walk. He stopped off to give Sandy a couple of understanding pats. "Well, you came home, eh?"

Only five more days left.

7

First thing I did next day was to make sure Sandy was tied up. I went down to the yard. Sandy was lying down. That should have tipped me off. "Hey, come on, boy. Let's go." Instead of barking and wagging his tail, he just lay there. His eyes looked sort of glassy. "Gee, are you sick?" Mom thought he was, not that she had ever seen a sick dog, but Sandy reminded her of me when I had the flu.

"We'd better have him checked out,"
she said and called to make an appointment
with the vet.

When we walked in the door, the waiting
room was packed with people and animals.
I held on to Sandy while Mom commanded
him to sit.

"Sit! Sit! Sandy, sit." Believe it or not,
he sat. The other people smiled at me, and

I smiled back. I guess they thought Sandy was my dog. In a way he was . . . for the week.

A dog was howling and barking in one of the private rooms. I wondered if animals react to those sounds the same way some people do in the dentist's office. One dog gave a weak bark, but Sandy just lay there.

We were there a half hour when the receptionist called his name. "Follow me, please," and she directed us into Room 2, where all three of us waited for the vet.

Dr. Abrams put Sandy on the table and began to examine him, almost the same way our doctor examines me. When he finished he didn't appear too concerned.

"Your dog seems to have a cold. When did he get his last injection?"

I didn't know. "Well, was he ever sick before?"

"I don't know. We're taking care of him

while a friend is away," I said.

"Well," said the vet, "let's see if we can make him better real soon." He was filling a long needle with fluid. Fortunately Sandy didn't know what was going to happen. When the vet stuck him with the needle, Sandy hardly moved a muscle. What a dog!

The vet gave us some pills to give him twice a day. "He'll be fine in a day or two."

When we went back out into the waiting room the other dogs stared at Sandy. It was almost as though they wanted a signal from him about what they should expect when it was their turn.

The technician showed us how to grab open Sandy's jaws in order to put the pill way back on his tongue.

When we got home we put Sandy in the den . . . "until he gets better," Mom said. "He must have caught cold from his adventure in the rain yesterday. Poor Sandy."

Someone should have been making a videotape of the next ten minutes. You wouldn't believe what went on as we tried to give Sandy his first pill. I grabbed his upper and lower jaw and separated them the way the technician showed us.

"Okay, Mom, toss the pill in back of his tongue. Mom! Let's go. For gosh sakes, put the pill in. I can't hold his mouth open forever. . . ."

Mom wanted to know, "What if he closes his jaws on my hand and severs a couple of fingers. . . ?"

I let go of Sandy's jaw. It snapped shut. Mom and I had to have a talk. "Look, he can't snap his jaws. I've got a stranglehold on them. Don't put your hand in his mouth. Just throw the pill in as far back as you can. Okay?"

I grabbed Sandy's jaw again and pulled

open his mouth. Sandy was really being very good about all this. Mom threw the pill inside. I released Sandy's jaw. Sandy spat the pill out on the rug.

"Mom, this time you open his mouth and let me try giving him the pill."

Mom gave it her best, but she didn't know where to squeeze to get his jaws open. Sandy was beginning to show signs of agitation.

"We better do this fast now or we won't be doing it at all, Mom."

I opened Sandy's mouth wide enough for Mom to deposit the pill. "Okay, now!" I shouted, and with the aim of a sharp-shooter, Mom succeeded.

I released Sandy's jaw, and you could see him swallowing the pill.

"Hurray! We did it! We did it!"

In the evening Mom gave Dad the opportunity of "pilling" Sandy. Dad made good on the first pitch. In bed that night I decided to become a vet when I grew up.

Now there were only four dog days left.

8

Sandy was much better the following day. He was no longer listless and was almost back to his old self.

"Why don't you go out with your friends today, and I'll take care of Sandy," Mom said. The idea intrigued me.

I called Danny. "Hey, what's doin'?"

"Nothin' much."

"Wanna bike ride to the cliffs?"

"Nah, Julia and I did that yesterday. Besides I'm goin' shopping for shoes today. But I'll see ya later this afternoon, okay?"

Mom was coming up from the basement. I must have surprised her because her face went pale.

"I have nothing to do," I complained. I realized my mistake the minute the words passed my lips. She gave me a verbal list of things I *could* do: Clean out the garage . . . sweep the walk . . . wash the dishes . . . read.

Reading seemed the least amount of effort. I had my own library of about thirty books, only half of which I had read. I closed my eyes and reached for a book. Lots of my decisions are made with my eyes closed — which shirt to wear, which homework to do first, which game to play.

I got comfortable in Dad's armchair and opened the first page. *The Mystery of the*. . . . The rest of the title had a food stain covering it. It looked like spaghetti sauce.

I was on page thirty when I heard a noise in the basement. "Mom, is that you?" No answer. "MOM?" I opened the door to the basement and slowly tiptoed down the stairs. "Mom," I whispered. Suddenly someone was in back of me.

"Hold it, kid. Don't turn around and you won't get hurt."

"Who are you? What are you doing here? Where's my mother?"

"This isn't a game show, kid, and I don't have to answer. This is a robbery." And he pushed me up the stairs and into the kitchen.

Mom was already tied up to a chair. "Now, you," the thief said to me, "be good, and nothin'll happen to youse." He slammed the door shut, or thought he did, and went up to the bedrooms.

Mom was all upset. I tried to calm her down. "It's gonna be okay. Don't worry. I'm here." Then an idea popped into my head. I began to move my chair around the kitchen a little at a time so as not to make any noise. When I was back-to-back with Mom's chair we tried to undo each other's knots.

Mine suddenly came loose, and I helped Mom. We quickly moved our chairs back and waited for the robber to return, wondering exactly what we could do.

The door slowly opened. "Don't shoot, Mister," I pleaded. "We won't tell the cops. We won't squeal. . . ."

I couldn't believe I was really saying all this trash. I could have saved myself all that embarrassment, because it was Sandy who had made his way undetected through the door. Thank goodness he knew enough to be quiet. But he was stupid enough to start licking my face.

"Hey. Cut that out! Go away! Stop it! Scram!" But as luck would have it Sandy didn't scram. And when the door opened again Sandy lunged for the thief, taking him completely by surprise.

The thief was knocked down, and his gun dropped to the floor. I reached for it while Sandy, teeth threatening, held the man at bay in the corner of the kitchen. "Mom, get on the phone and call the police. And tell them to bring a medal for a very special dog."

When the police came they handcuffed the intruder and led him away. Sandy barked his head off, he was so excited. "Sandy. Stop barking! Stop bar — "

"Wake up, Sweetie! Benjie, wake up! Are you all right? You must have had a bad dream."

I stretched. I must have fallen asleep while I was reading. But I bet even if it wasn't a dream, Sandy would have saved us. "Right, Sandy?" I gave him a pat.

The doorbell rang. It was Danny, wearing

his new shoes. "Wanna come to my house and play some video games?"

Mom offered to walk Sandy, and I ended up having dinner at Danny's house. I discovered that he can't get up from the table till he eats his string beans, either. (What is it with parents and string beans?) Before I left we decided to go fishing the following morning. "See you at eight," I said.

Three days to go.

9

"**M**a, where's my fishing rod? I can't find it. . . . " My line was all tangled in knots, and I couldn't find a single fly. That touched off a ten-minute lecture about taking care of my things and putting them away where they belong. Mom was right, but neatness took so much time.

I looked all over the place for the rod, and would you believe it, I found it in the closet, where it belonged. I should have looked there first. "I found it, Mom," I shouted, knowing full well she wasn't looking for it anyway.

Now for the fly. But I decided to get dressed first. It was while I was looking for my shirt that I found the two quarters I lost last week, and while I was looking for my other sneaker I found the fishing fly. Three, as a matter of fact. If I've learned anything after all these years of living, it's never to look directly for a lost object. You'll never find it that way. Go figure.

"Mom, I'm going."

"What about Sandy?"

"I'm taking him with me, okay?"

"I don't see why not. Wait and I'll make you some sandwiches."

I gave the bag to Sandy, and he carried it all the way to the lake for me. Danny had Sally there, too, and both dogs romped about on the grass, barking and sparring and testing each other.

Danny and I sat on the dock, threw in our lines, and waited for the whoppers to bite. We talked about our teachers and the kids we knew, and then Danny said, "You know what? Heino's mother and father are getting a divorce. They aren't going to live together anymore."

"What's gonna happen to Heino? Besides, who told you that?"

"I heard my parents talking. Heino will stay here and live with his mother."

I felt bad, but at least Heino won't be moving away, and it'll be just like it's always been . . . except, I guess, for Heino.

My line suddenly gave a jerk. Whatever was at the end of it was thrashing about wildly.

I was trying to hold on to my end with all my might. I wanted to let go, but I couldn't, and the thing at the other end was not going to give in, either. Before I knew what was happening, I was jerked into the lake and dragged along until I was in water over my head. I let go of the tackle and cried, "Help! Help!"

I could dog-paddle a little and managed to keep myself afloat.

Danny and the two dogs were at the edge of the lake. Danny was yelling, "I can't swim, Benjie."

One of the dogs suddenly jumped into the water and swam toward me. It was Sandy.

He grabbed me by the shirt and began dragging me to shore. In the shallow water I was finally able to stand. I even found my fishing tackle. But the fish had gotten away.

I lay down on the grass and could see that Danny looked scared.

"Benjie, are you all right?" he kept repeating. "Are you? Say something."

I couldn't. I really felt fine but I must have been in a kind of shock, and words refused to pass my lips. I looked up into Danny's face and forced a smile to reassure him of my continued existence. His worried expression relaxed.

"Boy, you sure scared me. I thought you were a goner. . . . "

I suddenly felt hungry. I sat up and bit into my sandwich.

For a long time I didn't talk. I was doing a lot of thinking. . . . How my parents would cry if Danny brought them the news of my drowning . . . . How Mom would say it was all her fault and Dad would convince her it wasn't, like he always does. I thought about how much I loved them and how I'd never want them to get a divorce. Maybe if Heino almost drowned his parents would feel sorry and not get a divorce.

We waited until my clothes dried before going home. I couldn't decide if I should tell my parents what had happened or just leave it a secret between Sandy and me.

And that was day five — only two more days to go.

10

I took life easy the next day. Somehow, I felt different. Like a different person. Different from how I felt before the accident. Mr. Label would be home the next day, and Sandy would go back.

"Why so quiet?" Mom asked. "I hardly know you're in the house today. Is everything all right?"

"Sure, Ma. I just don't feel like making a lot of noise today. You know what I really feel like? I feel like cleaning up my closet and toy chest."

"Have you got a fever, Benjie? Let me feel your head."

"I'm fine, Ma, honest. I just think that it's time to get rid of some of my baby toys and stuff."

"Maybe not, Benjie."

"But you're always yelling at me to do it."

"Well, that was then. But now it seems I'm going to have a baby."

You could have knocked me down with a feather. "A *baby!* You're going to have a baby? When did you find out?"

"Yesterday, while you and Sandy were at the lake. The doctor says to expect it in about seven months . . . probably next February."

I wasn't sure just how to react. After all no one ever confronted me with a baby before. All I could say was, "Wow! Gee whiz. A baby!" And I ran over and hugged and kissed Mom until she almost fell off the chair. "It would be nice if you'd think about sharing your room until we can add on another one to the house," she said.

I went into my room and lay down on my bed. What a week of happenings!

I jumped up again and began separating the toys — mine and the baby's. Then I went to look for a carton. I started going down to the basement. Mom stopped me and said I'd find a carton in the garage. I pasted some contact paper around it and the box looked great. Then I wrote the word *baby* all over the sides.

Next was my closet. When I opened the door I just wanted to close it again. But I took a deep breath and dumped everything into the middle of the rug. Slowly, one by one, I separated my shirts from my sports equipment, my socks from my trains, my papers and notebooks from under my shoes. You wouldn't believe all the things I found that had been missing for months . . . maybe years. There was even George's baseball bat that I had sworn I had given back to him.

Sandy suddenly appeared in the doorway with a leash in his mouth.

"Be right with you, Pal."

And so day six came to an end.

11

Well, today is day seven. Mr. Label will be back tonight. I went into Mom's room. She was putting a new outlet into the wall. "This one's dead," she said, holding it up. "The week certainly went fast, Benjie, and you don't look any the worse for it. Now you can have all that time you spent on Sandy for yourself."

Mom finished screwing in the outlet and put the power back on. "I have an idea

. . . why don't you invite some of your friends over, and we'll have a farewell party for Sandy?"

I made a lot of phone calls, and by the time the party began eight people had arrived — the whole baseball team.

Sandy never had so many bones at once in his life. He'd pick one up, chew it, drop it, and then pick up another . . . nine bones in all. He didn't sit still for a minute.

We played "tie the ribbon on Sandy's tail" and hide-and-seek. Sandy was it. He always found me first.

When the food was ready we all sat down at the table — yes, including Sandy — and ate our ice cream and cookies. Then we all toasted Sandy with lemonade: "To Sandy, the greatest dog in the world." Danny stood on his chair. "To Sandy, my dog's best friend."

Max was next. He and Leon had made
up a poem:

"We think you're swell.
We think you're smart.
We love you a lot.
With all our heart.
Hooray!"

Then I got up. "I just made up a poem:
I want you to know.
I'll miss you so."

60

And we guzzled down the rest of our lemonade.

By four o'clock everyone had left.

By five o'clock it was time to take Sandy back to Mr. Label. The day I couldn't wait for was here. Even the hour.

I put the leash on Sandy. Mom patted

him on the back. "Good-bye, Sandy," she said. I thought I saw a tear in the corner of her eye.

Sandy's tail was wagging like crazy. Out the door he bolted, and I had all I could do to hold on. Danny, as was all too common now, was out with Sally. "We'll walk you over," he said.

The car was in the driveway at Mr. Label's house. "I guess they're home."

"They must be," Danny said.

Even Sandy must have known. He started to bark like crazy. The front door opened, and Mr. Label came running out.

"Sandy! Good boy!" Was Sandy ever glad to see him! "I hope he wasn't too much trouble for you, Benjie."

"No, sir, no trouble at all. He was great. We had a terrific time." And then I heard myself say it. "I'm going to miss Sandy."

"Come visit him anytime, Benjie."

12

If I was glad the week was over, then why was I feeling so sad? I'd get over it as soon as I got home, I was sure. But I didn't.

Mom was taking things out of the closet.

"Benjie, will you bring me the carton in back of the stairs in the basement?"

I found it right away, but it wasn't empty. Something was inside. It scared me. A family of mice or even rats could be in there! But then I heard a bark, and I was smart enough to know that mice and rats don't bark. Dogs do.

"*Dogs?*" I reached into the box and lifted out a small, shivering puppy. "Mom!" I cried. "Mommmm. . . Look what I found in the basement!"

"Happy birthday, Benjie. Your father and I hope you'll want to keep him. He's a pure thoroughbred."

I had a feeling I was being tricked, but I didn't care. I wanted this dog more than anything. I ran outside to show the kids my new dog, Sandy. Only Sergio was around. Poor guy. He hasn't got a dog. He doesn't know what he's missing.

"Coming to practice tomorrow, Benjie?" he asked.

"Yeah, yeah," I said. "I'll be there with my dog."

So what else is new?